Discard

The Butterflies Come

BY LEO POLITI

CHARLES SCRIBNER'S SONS

NEW YORK

NOTE

The nature facts of this story are true.

Every year the Monarch butterflies take long journeys south to spend the winter. They travel all over the United States, but in Pacific Grove, on the Monterey Peninsula in California, they come to the same trees in thousands, each year.

In spring the butterflies go north. As they go, they lay their eggs on the milkweed plant, then their life is over. Caterpillars hatch from the eggs and later these become orange-colored Monarch butterflies. The butterflies return in the fall to the same butterfly trees.

11 13 15 17 19 RD/C 20 18 16 14 12

SBN 684-12348-7

The
Butterflies
Come

Stephen and Lucia lived on the Monterey
Peninsula by the blue Pacific Ocean.
On sunny days they liked to go down
and play by the sea.

On stormy days, safe indoors, they liked to watch the angry waves rise and splash against the rocks. When the storm was over, they wondered at the beautiful rainbow arched across the sky.

There were some days when clouds of mist rose and hid the sea. Sometimes the clouds were so close that Stephen and Lucia felt they could almost walk over them.

When Stephen went to school, Lucia was not lonely at home, because she made friends with the birds and animals from the nearby woods.

In the morning she was awakened by the noisy bluejays playing in the branches by her window. She knew them and called them by name.

Every day a mother and baby deer came near the house. At first the baby deer's thin legs were wobbly and he could hardly stand up.

Lucia loved him. She saved bits of bread and was happy when the deer came to eat from her hands. They were timid, though, and soon ran away into the woods. They stopped to look back now and then as they hid behind bushes and tree trunks.

Lucia thought they wanted to play hide-and-seek.

Sometimes little black and white skunks came through the woods. Lucia knew it was best to keep far away from them!

Lucia made friends with the gray squirrels that lived in the pine trees.

One day she found a lost baby squirrel.

She took him home and fed him warm milk. Then in a box she made him a bed lined with pine needles and Spanish moss.

Lucia named the squirrel Coco. He was friendly and loved her. But one day, when he was a little bigger, he ran off into the woods.

Lucia was sad because she thought he would never come back.

But although she did not forget Coco, soon Lucia had some new friends.

In the fall of the year, the first Monarch butterflies came to the Monterey Peninsula.

The Monarchs are beautiful orange-red butterflies. They come every year to spend the winter.

Lucia liked to watch them. They danced and fluttered everywhere: in the flower gardens, along the streets, even through the houses, if doors and windows were open.

By the middle of October the butterflies began to come in groups.

One day, as Stephen and Lucia were playing in the garden, they saw a strange cloud over the bay. As it came nearer they could see it was a cloud of thousands of orange butterflies glittering in the sunlight. As they passed overhead, Stephen and Lucia could hear the faint rustling sound of countless wings.

Children from other houses ran out to see. Even the birds and little animals of the woods watched with wonder. The golden cloud went through the trees and disappeared on the other side of the hill.

"Those are the Monarch butterflies on their way to the butterfly trees," said Stephen.

"What are the butterfly trees?" asked Lucia.

"The butterfly trees are where the Monarch butterflies live, and they are on the other side of the hill."

"I wish I could see them."

Mother said that Stephen could take Lucia to the trees. Lucia was very excited.

The children walked along the winding road which led through the woods to the butterfly trees. Now and then they passed charming little houses with gardens, nestling among the green trees. In every garden a few butterflies danced among the flowers.

Then Stephen and Lucia left the winding road and took a short cut through the woods. It was more fun to go that way. Above them the branches of the trees made a green canopy through which they could hardly see the sky. It was like going through a real forest.

As they sat on a log to rest, Stephen told Lucia about the butterflies. "They came here a long, long time ago. Indians lived in these woods near the butterfly trees. And every year the butterflies came in the fall and left in the spring—just as they do now.

The Indians were happy when the butterflies came to Pacific Grove. They beat on their drums and danced with joy, because they thought the butterflies brought good luck when they came. There would be good crops, and times of peace and plenty.

"And all through the winter months the Indians liked to do their work as the lovely butterflies fluttered around them."

"I wish the Indians were here now," said Lucia.

As they walked on, Stephen told Lucia more about the butterflies.

"Just think, Lucia, they come all the way from Canada, and they are such little things to travel so far. But the real mystery is—how they find their way back to a place they've never been before. The old ones live only a few months—and everyone wonders what guides the young ones back to the butterfly trees."

"If only the butterflies could talk, they could tell us," said Lucia.

"Yes, wouldn't it be nice if they could talk and tell us all the interesting things they've seen on their way?"

At last Stephen and Lucia came to the butterfly trees.

"Be very quiet, Lucia," Stephen told her. "We must not frighten them."

At first Lucia did not see the butterflies, though almost every branch of every tree was filled with

them. For when the butterflies rest and close
their wings, the undersides of the wings
look like clusters of dried leaves.

Suddenly a playful squirrel leaped from one branch
to another. In a moment thousands of butterflies rose
in the air. It was a glorious sight. The golden orange
of their open wings sparkled in the sunlight that
came through the trees. Lucia could not believe her
eyes.

"It's really butterfly land!" she thought.

When the squirrel had gone, some butterflies went back to the trees, others fluttered about. A few of them alighted on Lucia as if they had come to greet her. They were attracted by her bright-colored sweater. One even flew onto Stephen's hand.

"Look, Lucia, how lovely and friendly they are," whispered Stephen as he held the butterfly very gently, without touching its delicate wings.

Like Stephen and Lucia, the people of Pacific Grove are very kind to the butterflies. They love them so well that every year they celebrate their arrival with a gay Butterfly Festival.

Stephen had been at the festival the year before, so he told Lucia all about the children's Butterfly Parade. Boys and girls, dressed in costumes which tell the story of the Monarch butterfly, marched up and down the streets of the town.

"The girls look lovely in their butterfly dresses," Stephen said. "Some of them are dressed like the flowers the butterflies love best to visit."

As they went back, Stephen told of all the fun and excitement caused by the make-believe Monarch caterpillar in the parade. It was propelled by the legs of many children. He said his were the last pair of legs at the back of the caterpillar.

Lucia laughed when Stephen told her that once he fell down and dragged other children down with him. It seemed as if the whole caterpillar would fall. But luckily this did not happen. The caterpillar was set right again and marched on.

"I wish I had a butterfly dress and could be in the parade," Lucia sighed.

Just then the children heard a little noise in the bushes. What could it be?

They stood still to look—and there was a gray squirrel. It leaped right into Lucia's arms.

"Coco, Coco! I am so glad to see you!" cried Lucia. Then she said to Stephen:

"How could Coco find us way out here in the woods?"

"I think there is something that looks after little creatures and guides them to where they wish to be," said Stephen. "We know there is something that guides the butterflies back to the butterfly trees."

Coco climbed up on Lucia's shoulder and leaned his face against her cheek. Soon the three of them were back in their own garden.

Mother greeted them with a surprise. While they were away, she had finished the Indian suit she had been working on for Stephen to wear in the parade, and for Lucia she had made lovely butterfly wings to wear with her yellow dress. For Coco she had some nuts.

Stephen and Lucia were so happy and excited that they hugged their mother many times.

"Let's put on our costumes and have a play," Stephen said. "Lucia, you be a butterfly and I'll be an Indian and beat on my drum."

So Lucia danced in the garden and fluttered happily from flower to flower.

Stephen beat softly on his drum as the old-time Indians did when the butterflies arrived. As Lucia danced he chanted:

"They have come! They have come—bringing peace, bringing plenty."

The birds and animals of the woods came to watch.

Butterflies, attracted by Lucia's bright costume, came to flutter and dance around her.

Stephen and Lucia went to bed early that evening, so they could get up early for the festival next day. Mother gently fixed the covers over her children, kissed them goodnight and turned off the light.

Soon Stephen and Lucia were sound asleep.

Out in the woods the little animals, the birds and the butterflies were asleep, too. All was silent except for the pleasant murmur of the waves from the sea.